To my wife, Amanda, who made me wait forever for our first date.
- Mr. Jay

New Paige Press, LLC
NewPaigePress.com

ISBN 978-1-7345980-5-6

Printed and bound in China

New Paige Press provides special discounts when purchased in larger volumes for premiums and promotional purposes, as well as for fundraising and educational use. Custom editions can also be created for special purposes. In addition, supplemental teaching material can be provided upon request. For more information, please visit NewPaigePress.com

New Paige Press is an imprint of
LYRIC & STONE
PUBLISHING

PATRICK PICKLEBOTTOM
AND THE LONGEST WAIT

Story by
Mr. Jay

Artwork by
Gary Wilkinson

For young Patrick Picklebottom,
who loved books most of all,
it was exciting to read what was up on the wall.
The sign said that story time's 'round five o'clock –
A cute little tale, 'bout a flat-sided rock.
It's supposed to be good – he had heard a review,
but he was two hours early, with nothing to do.

So he
sat.

And
he
waited.

And he waited some more.
More bored, more impatient, than ever before.

Was it five yet? He looked at the clock just to see,
but oh no! It was only two minutes past three.
It felt like a week had already gone by –
and for a moment he thought
he might break down and cry.

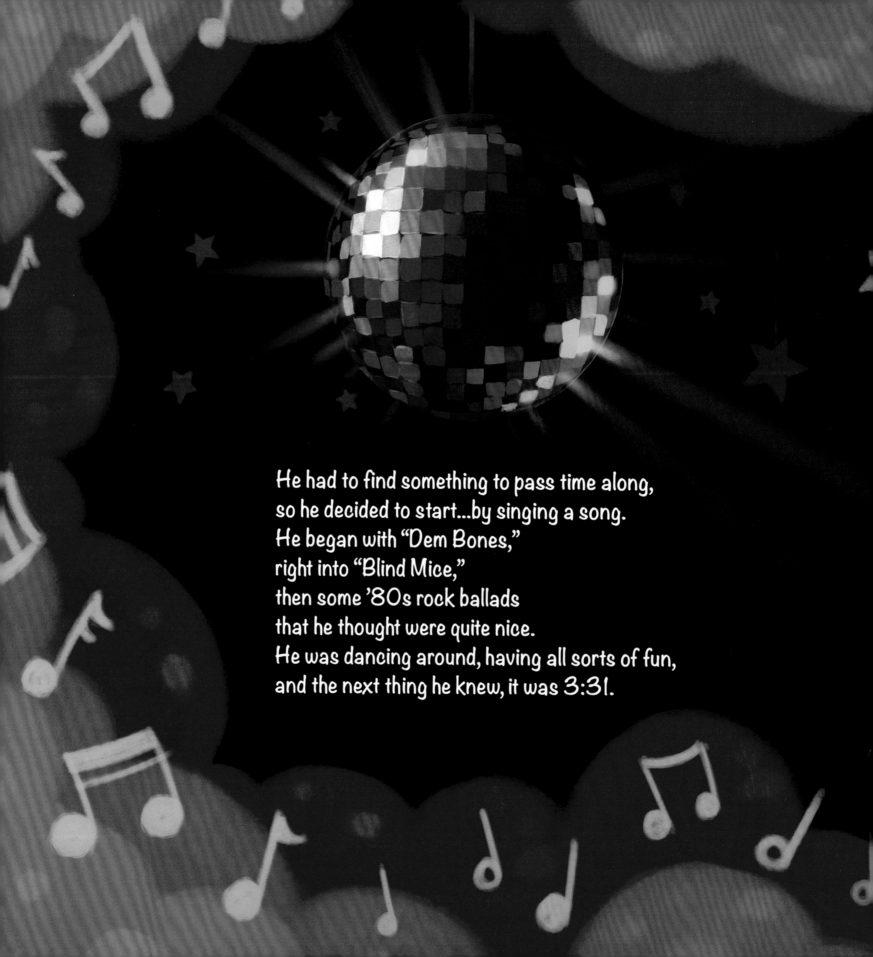

He had to find something to pass time along,
so he decided to start...by singing a song.
He began with "Dem Bones,"
right into "Blind Mice,"
then some '80s rock ballads
that he thought were quite nice.
He was dancing around, having all sorts of fun,
and the next thing he knew, it was 3:31.

Patrick sang all his songs
and his dancing was through,
so he set out to find something
new he could do.
So he wrote a short poem,
about a little green elf –
not a bad piece of work
(if he said so himself):

The green little
sat up on a s
and didn't have much to
He chewed on his
and then wondered "wh
So he ate his delicious green

So it wasn't that great,
and he'd have written some more,
but he glanced at the clock,
and it was ten after four!

The next thing he did was to find some old chalk,
and he drew a bright sun, some clouds, and a hawk,
soaring the sky 'bove a field and a lake
and then, for no reason, he drew a big cake.
It was chocolate with frosting and swirly red lines,
and big smiley faces and star-shaped designs.

Then he drew a fast car and pretended to race,
before drawing a rocket and flying through space.
A small castle here, and a dinosaur there,
and a chess game between a fern and a bear.
He drew a small monster biting somebody's nose,
and then a fat bug wearing oversized clothes.

Patrick stared up at the world he'd created –
all the things he had made in the time he had waited.

The next thing he knew, it was twenty past five,
but story time had simply failed to arrive.
He looked at the sign to figure out why,
and smiled to himself with a wry little sigh.

The time was at five,
but the day was *tomorrow*...
though he didn't feel anger,
annoyance, or sorrow.

He'd simply come back,
and he wouldn't be late –
precisely at three,
to enjoy his long wait.